Joanne Oppenheim

You Can't Catch Me!

Illustrations by Andrew Shachat

Houghton Mifflin Company   Boston   1986

4   W

To my parents, for their support and understanding.

A.S.

To Kate, welcome!

J.O.

Library of Congress Cataloging-in-Publication Data

Oppenheim, Joanne.
 You can't catch me!

 Summary: A pesky black fly taunts all the animals, boasting that they cannot
catch him, until he bothers one animal too many.
 [1. Flies—Fiction. 2. Animals—Fiction. 3. Stories in rhyme]
 I. Shachat, Andrew, ill. II. Title.
PZ8.3.0615Yo   1986   [E]   86-7211
ISBN 0-395-41452-0

Printed in Japan

DNP   10   9   8   7   6   5   4   3   2   1

There once was a fly,

a pesky black fly,

no bigger or smaller

than most.

And this buzzy black fly

was a bothersome fly

who loved to tease and boast. "No matter how hard you try

try

try

you can't catch me!"

called the pesky

black

fly.

He bothered a cow
who was taking a nap.
With her tufted tail
she gave him a slap!

"You can't catch me!"

called the pesky black fly.

"No matter how hard you try

try

try!"

He bothered a goat

who lowered his head,

stuck out his horns,

and clearly said, "I swear by the hair on my chinny

chin

chin

I'll catch you, fly, and do you in!"

"You can't," laughed the fly,

"Your horns won't do!

I flew from the cow,

and I'll fly from you, too!

No matter how hard you try

try

try

you can't catch me!"

called the pesky black fly.

He pestered a horse,
all dappled and gray,
who was munching a lunch
of timothy hay.
Horse shook his head
and stomped the ground
and whinnied an angry horse's sound.

"I'll get you, fly!"
Then he started to trot.
But the fly called back,
"Oh, no, you will not!
I flew from the goat
and I flew from the cow.
They couldn't catch me
and you won't now!

No matter how hard you try

try

try

you can't catch me!"

called the pesky black fly.

He bothered a fox

who bared his teeth

and growled, "Pesky fly, you'll come to grief!"

"Try," said the fly, "but you'll
fail, of course.
The cow did,
the goat did,
and so did the horse.
No matter how hard you try
try
try
you can't catch me!"
called the pesky black
fly.

He buzzed 'round a bear
who was snatching a hive.
"Woof!" growled bear,
"I'll eat you alive!"

"I dare you, bear!

I'm faster than you.

I'm faster than cow

goat

horse

and fox, too!

No matter how hard you try

try

try

you can't catch me!"

called the pesky black fly.

He pestered a pig

who was slurping his slop.

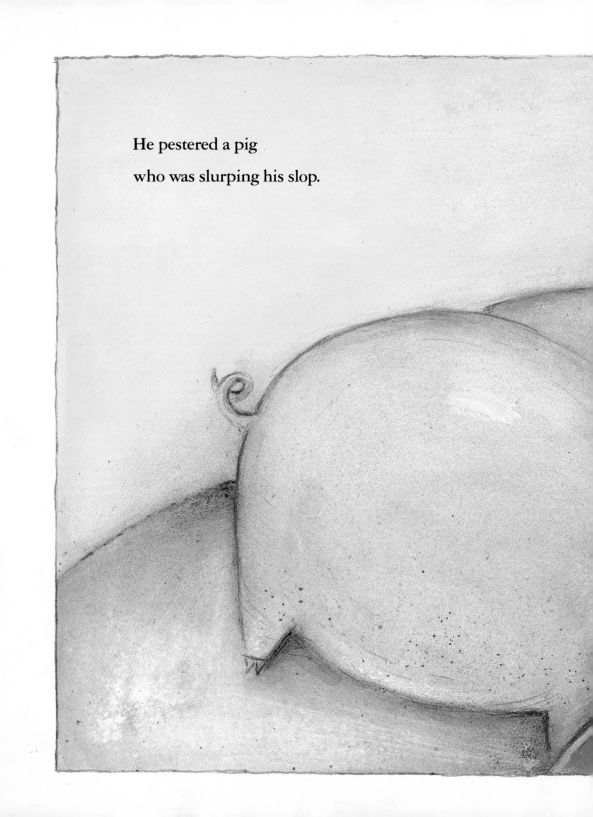

That fat pig squealed, "Now stop

                            stop

                            stop

or I'll flatten you, fly,

with my stout pink snout!"

"Try!" laughed the fly,

"but I have no doubt

you won't catch me!"

Then he started to shout.

"No matter how hard you try

try

try

you can't catch me!"

called the pesky black

fly.

He pestered the sheep

and their dear little lambs

till one ram shouted, "Scram, fly, scram!

Or I'll lead a stampede of my sisters and brothers!"

"Ha!" laughed the fly.
"You're just like the others!
No matter how hard you try

                    try

                    try

you can't catch me!"

        called the pesky black fly.

By nighttime the fly

found a rock for a bed,

but while he was sleeping

the rock grew a head . . .

A little green head

with wide-opened eyes

that looked at the fly

in great surprise.

"You can't," the fly started . . .

But that's all he said.

Zap! went the turtle,

and in went his head!

And that was the end

of the bothersome fly.

Good-bye,

pesky fly,

Good-bye!

Good-bye!